The Story of Joe, The Donkey Who Flew to Jamaica

Written by *Dr Elisabeth D. Svendsen M B E*
Illustrated by *Tom Morse-Brown*

Whittet Books

First published 1997
© 1997 by Elisabeth D. Svendsen M B E
Whittet Books Ltd, 18 Anley Road W14 OBY

Illustrations © 1997 by Tom Morse-Brown

The Donkey Sanctuary is at Sidmouth Devon EX10 0NU

Tel: (01395) 578222

Fax: (01395) 579266

Registered Charity No. 264818

Printed in Hong Kong by Wing King Tong

ISBN 1 873580 36 3

Introduction

This little story is based on fact, although, for obvious reasons, names have been changed!

It will give British children an insight into the lives of their counterparts in Jamaica, and a practical way they can help in the education of those less fortunate than themselves.

Each copy purchased in the U.K. will enable a free copy to be sent to a school in Jamaica. Many schools in Jamaica are desperately short of teaching materials and the book will be very educational; perhaps even more important to me is the message of the book – the only problems of donkeys are the problems that humans cause!

I hope you enjoy the book, and think of the pleasure it will bring in tiny villages and towns in Jamaica.

Dr Elisabeth D. Svendsen M B E

The Story of Joe, The Donkey Who Flew to Jamaica

Joe was born on a small island called Grand Turk in the Caribbean Sea. In the old days the island had been used to supply salt to other countries, so much of the island had big lakes where the sand and salt had been dug out. There were very few trees, and most of the island was covered with thorny shrubs. It was very dry!

Joe's grandfather had worked at the salt diggings, but when the trade stopped, like many other donkeys, he had been turned away to fend for himself, as his owners could no longer afford to keep him. By the time Joe was born, his family had been living wild for some time.

Joe had learned how to

feed himself by searching out small patches of grass but, far more often, he wandered into the town to see what he could find in the dustbins and on the rubbish dumps. This was not always easy – sometimes groups of little boys would chase the donkeys and throw stones at them. If finding food was difficult, finding water was an even bigger problem. It hardly ever rained and sometimes he and his friends became quite desperately thirsty.

When Joe was nearly four years old things became really bad. He and his friends had drunk no water for days. One of them was so desperate he went down to the sea and took long, long gulps of the salty water. Before very long he was rolling on the sand in agony with stomach ache!

Joe decided he wouldn't do that! He did have a good idea, however. Every single house had a water tank in the garden, and every time it rained in the rainy season the people saved every drop of water from their roofs by letting it run through pipes into the garden tank.

Early one morning Joe and his friends stood quietly together in someone's garden. They could smell the water in the tank but they were not sure how to get at it! Naughty Joe decided that if they all worked together and kicked the pipe from the tank, the water might come out.

"Come on everybody – KICK!" brayed Joe –

and they did. To their joy the pipe broke away and gallons of lovely sweet water poured onto the ground. The donkeys drank and drank – they were SO happy, but not for long. Oh dear! Their braying had woken the family and suddenly the garden was full of cross people, all shouting at the donkeys! Joe and his friends galloped away. The donkeys were happy but they really had caused a problem.

"The donkeys must go," said the Minister. "We don't have enough water for ourselves and the donkeys, and they are such a nuisance coming into the town." Sadly the people agreed – but what should they do with them?

Luckily they had heard of someone in England who helped donkeys in trouble and they contacted The International Donkey Protection Trust. Dr Svendsen (known as "Mother" to everyone) went out to visit with June, who helped her, and Andrew the vet.

Firstly they met the government ministers, then they met some kind people who loved the donkeys and gave them water and food when they could. Finally they met Joe and his friends!

They decided to make a Pound – a place where a shelter could be built and the donkeys could be cared for and given water to drink. This was done,

and on the day the Pound opened many of the little
boys in the town gathered together to round up
the donkeys. Joe and his friends found it great fun
– they really enjoyed the chase, but by nightfall

they had been shut into the Pound.

It was quite a change for Joe – he was used to running free, and by the morning he had managed to push and pull his way out of the Pound and had galloped off – naughty Joe!

The same thing kept happening night after night. Joe and his friends did not like the Pound and every time they were caught they managed to escape again!

June and Andrew had been back to see that all was well, and they were very worried that the donkeys were not happy in the Pound. They had a meeting with Mother and they decided that perhaps some of the donkeys would be happier on another island – but which one?

Andrew had lived on the beautiful island of Jamaica for many years, so he went there to see if they would give a nice home to some of the donkeys. The people of Jamaica agreed!

Joe and his friends had become used to being caught and put in the Pound. They knew it was easy to escape, so one morning when the boys caught them they did not worry. However, before they had the chance to escape again, two strange ladies appeared. They quickly put head collars on Joe and some of his friends, and before the donkeys were really sure what was happening, the ladies were leading them out of the Pound and into a large airy shed. Despite all their attempts, this time they could not escape, so they settled down and soon

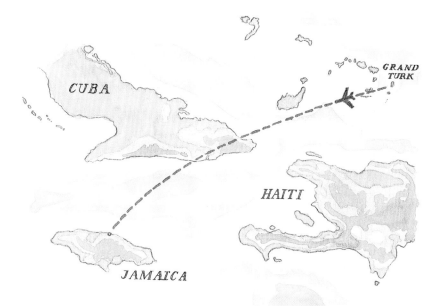

From Grand Turk to Jamaica

began to enjoy feeling kind hands brushing them, being fed lovely hay and being given as much water as they could drink – what a change from feeling hungry and thirsty and having stones thrown at them! But one day it all changed again, and a really exciting adventure began!

Joe had been pleased to see June and Andrew,

13

and especially pleased when one morning, with all the ladies, they were taken out for a long walk. But where to? Their ears pricked up as they heard strange noises. They were led across a hard tarmac path, and there was the biggest bird they had ever seen! The donkeys had never seen an aeroplane before, but because June and Andrew and the ladies

did not seem frightened, they decided it must be all right.

Joe and his friends were led into a large metal box, and suddenly Joe had to brace his little legs together as the box lifted into the air! He looked over the side and could see everyone smiling and waving at him. The box moved forward, the door

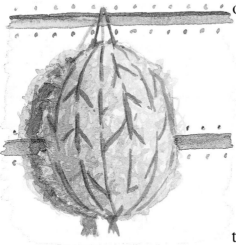

opened and he and his friends walked into the aeroplane! It was a lovely large compartment and there was a net full of fresh hay in front of them.

Once the door of the aeroplane had shut, Joe heard a loud noise and suddenly he realised the aeroplane was moving! Up, up it went and he really enjoyed the strange movement. He brayed happily to Andrew, who came to see the donkeys were all right, and then, not bothering about anything, Joe started to tackle the hay net.

It seemed no time before the aeroplane landed and, as the doors opened, Joe peered out to see where he was. There was a lovely spicy smell, the sun was shining, and Andrew told them all that

they were in Jamaica.

It was so exciting. They couldn't wait to see where they were going and couldn't believe the beautiful place they were taken to – it was paradise! There were lush green trees, which Joe had never seen before, a river bed which actually had water running in it and lots and lots of fresh grass – a dream for Joe! He decided he would never escape from here!

Mother had agreed that, once the donkeys had settled on the island, they could be "adopted" by families who needed them. After a few weeks, Andrew arranged for Joe to go to a very nice family in a little village in the Parish of St Ann.

Joe loved his new family! There were five children – Leonard, the eldest, Grace, Rose, Doret and Joseph. They lived in a little wooden house with a zinc roof. Around the roof was a bamboo guttering which collected the rainwater during the rainy season and stored it in a tank in the garden.

Inside the house there were just two rooms; all the children slept in one room and their parents slept in the other.

To Joe's delight the kitchen was outside, where the family sat at benches to eat their meals. He soon found that, if he brayed loudly enough, Leonard would run across to his little paddock,

which had a rickety wooden fence, and offer him a little titbit.

It was Leonard's job to look after Joe, and every morning he would get up at 5 o'clock and, because there was no running water in the house, he would go to the village pump with a large bucket to bring water back to thirsty Joe. Whilst Joe drank it, Leonard would brush him. He didn't have a proper brush, so he made a sort of curry comb from an empty sardine can with holes bored in it. It was a bit like a grater, but Leonard used it gently so that it pulled all the burrs and knots from Joe's coat.

By six o'clock the family were sitting having breakfast, and if Joe was lucky

he got a quick lick at the children's porridge bowls!
Sometimes, for a treat, he was allowed a little sip
of sersey tea – it was made from a vine with a yellow
fruit and was supposed to be good for everybody.

Then it was time for Joe to have a saddle, made
of plaited banana leaves, placed on his back, and
with Leonard leading him, they followed

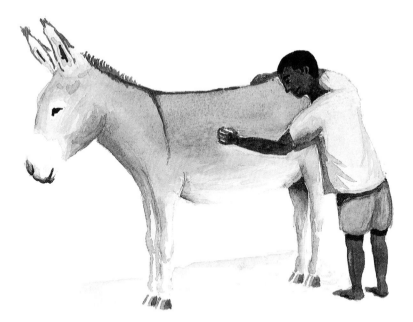

Leonard's father to go to work in the fields. The family's field was about four miles away from their home, and was about half an acre in size. During the school holidays and at weekends boys had to go to the fields to work with their fathers and uncles.

Sersey fruit

Some fields were planted with bananas, some with yams and corn in the autumn. All the fields had lime, orange, grapefruit and breadfruit trees for the families' use, and usually a little tobacco patch in the middle for the grandfathers!

When they arrived at the field, Joe was tied

A saddle made of plaited banana leaves

under a tree, as he didn't have to work during the day, and he watched happily as Leonard made up a fire. During the morning Leonard put a piece of corned pork in a pot over the blaze and, when it was half cooked, he added yams and dumplings, which everyone ate happily at lunchtime.

At the end of the day Joe found himself being

loaded up with produce and a large "goadie" which held drinking water for the family. Then, as a special treat he was offered a large piece of squashy fruit. It was called jack fruit and smelled terrible, but Joe loved it!

Happy day followed happy day, but one terrible day it all changed! Leonard had been feeling poorly for some time and on this particular Monday

Goadie

morning he felt too tired and sick to get up. No one came to see Joe, no one brought him water and no one let him lick a porridge bowl. The day wore on and the family were so worried about Leonard that they forgot all about Joe.

He became more and more hungry and more and more thirsty and by the next morning, whilst it was still dark, he knew what he had to do. Naughty Joe – he had always managed to break out of the Pound, and he soon pushed the rickety wooden fence down and trotted up to the house. He remembered his trick with the water tank in Grand Turk and decided that if no one would give him a drink

Jack fruit

of water he would have to get it himself.

Thump, thump, thump – his little hooves banged against the bamboo piping, making a terrible noise. He had forgotten that he didn't have his friends to help him. The noise woke up all the family, and everyone rushed out shouting, afraid that they were being burgled or attacked. Father had a big stick with him in case he needed it to protect his family.

Poor Joe – he was surrounded, and everyone looked so cross. He hung his head in shame and tried to become invisible. Suddenly everything changed – Leonard had come out to see what was happening, and he was better! He rushed up to

Breadfruit

Joe and threw his arms around his neck. "Oh Joe,
I'm so sorry. No one gave you any water. That's
why you were being so naughty ... poor Joe."

Suddenly all the family were saying they were
sorry for forgetting Joe, and a big tear slid down
his cheek. Leonard walked him back to his
paddock, Father mended the rickety wooden fence

and Doret ran all the way to the village pump to fetch Joe a bucket of water.

I don't think the family will ever forget Joe again, and I don't think Joe will ever be a naughty donkey again for the rest of his life!